Super Pocoyo

Adapted by Kristen L. Depken
Illustrated by Federico Pérez Moreno

 A GOLDEN BOOK • NEW YORK

POCOYO ™ © 2005–2013 Zinkia Entertainment, S.A. The POCOYO™ series, characters, and logos are trademarks of Zinkia Entertainment and are used only under license. All rights reserved. Published in the United States by Golden Books, an imprint of Random House Children's Books, a division of Random House, Inc., 1745 Broadway, New York, NY 10019, and in Canada by Random House of Canada Limited, Toronto, in conjunction with Disney Enterprises, Inc. Golden Books, A Golden Book, A Little Golden Book, the G colophon, and the distinctive gold spine are registered trademarks of Random House, Inc.
ISBN: 978-0-307-98160-8
randomhouse.com/kids
www.pocoyo.com
Printed in the United States of America
10 9 8 7 6 5 4 3 2 1

Hello, Pocoyo! Oh, wait—Pocoyo is not himself today.

He's Super Pocoyo!

Super Pocoyo wears a cape, a mask, and the letter *P*. He is a brave superhero who is always ready to help.

Super Pocoyo looks around.
Who does he see first?

Pato! He is
watering a flower.

Super Pocoyo will help the flower!

Super Pocoyo covers the flower
with a trash can.
    Pato does not think Super Pocoyo
was very helpful.

Super Pocoyo has an idea. Pato can be
Super Pato! They will make a great team.
What will their first mission be?

"Help friends!" shouts Super Pocoyo.
Pato agrees. He will make sure Super
Pocoyo gives the right kind of help.

Super Pocoyo uses his super vision and
spots someone who needs help.
Who is it?

Sleepy Bird!

"Stuck!" cries Super Pocoyo.

Pato tries to tell Super Pocoyo that Sleepy Bird is just taking a nap. But Super Pocoyo wants to help her anyway.

Super Pocoyo climbs up, up, up
to Sleepy Bird's nest. Then he
grabs Sleepy Bird and tugs . . .

and tugs . . .

. . . until Sleepy Bird **pops** out of her nest and lands on the ground.
Sleepy Bird wishes she were still asleep.

Super Pocoyo sees another friend to help!
Who is it?

Loula! She is
digging a hole.

Super Pocoyo uses his superpowers to fill in Loula's hole. He uses Super Pato, too.
Loula is not happy. She has been digging that hole all day!

Super Pocoyo sees another person to help.
Who is it?

Elly!
She is in a hammock.

"Elly's stuck!" shouts Super Pocoyo. Super Pato tries to tell Super Pocoyo that Elly is just resting. But Super Pocoyo won't listen.

Super Pocoyo runs to Elly. **Ta-da!**
Elly is so startled, she falls right out
of her hammock!

Elly is not happy with Super Pocoyo.

In fact, none of Super Pocoyo's friends are very happy with him.

Super Pocoyo was just trying to help,
but all he did was make everyone angry.
Super Pocoyo does not feel very super
anymore.

Can anyone cheer Pocoyo up?
Pato can!

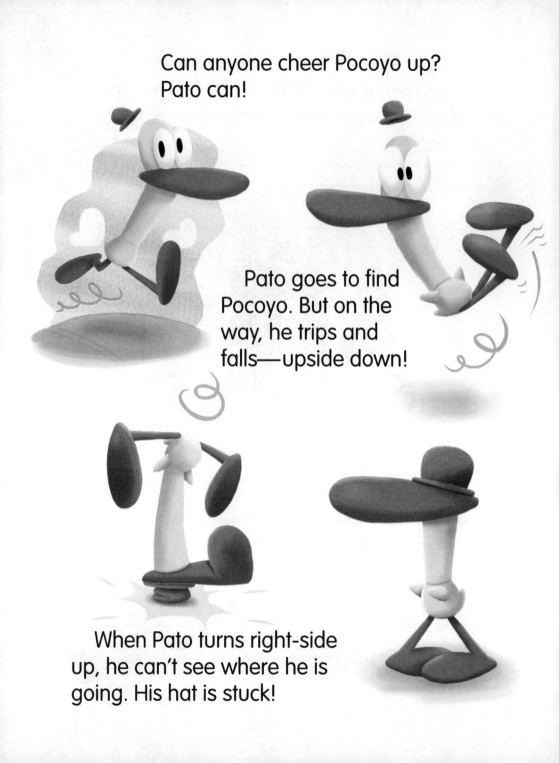

Pato goes to find
Pocoyo. But on the
way, he trips and
falls—upside down!

When Pato turns right-side
up, he can't see where he is
going. His hat is stuck!

Elly, Sleepy Bird, and Loula try to help Pato. But it is no use!

Who can help Pato now?

Super Pocoyo!

Super Pocoyo arrives just in time to get Pato's hat unstuck. Thank goodness Super Pocoyo was there to help!

Hooray for friends!

Hooray for Super Pocoyo!